HERO, TOFFER AND WALLABY

Hero, Toffer and Wallaby

Malachy Doyle

Illustrated by
Jan Nesbitt

First Impression—2000

ISBN 1 85902 845 4

© text: Malachy Doyle
© illustrations: Jan Nesbitt

This volume is published with the support of the
Arts Council of Wales.

Printed in Wales at
Gomer Press, Llandysul, Ceredigion SA44 4QL

for Isabel and Ryan

Chapter 1

As soon as the half-past three bell went, Hero, Toffer and Wallaby were off. Walking as quick as you can without running, out of the school and across the playground. Running as quick as you can without tripping, down Trem yr Allt.

Stopping off at number 12, just long enough to throw in a schoolbag, shout, 'Hi Mam, I'm off up The Mountain with Hero and Wallaby,' and grab three packets of crisps.

Past number 26, to chuck in a rucksack, yell, 'Hello Dad, just going up to The Wood with Toffer and Wallaby for a while,' and pocket a packet of chocolate biscuits.

Past number 54, the one on the end, dropping in long enough to toss in a sportsbag, leave a note saying, 'Up in The Den with Hero and Toffer, back by five.' And grab a can of coke from the fridge.

Then off up The Mountain. More of a hill than a mountain really but it's the nearest thing in Pentre so that's what they called it.

At the top of The Mountain there's The Wood. Less of a wood than a clump of trees, but who cares?

And in the middle of The Wood was The Den. Brilliant, it was. They'd only just finished making it. All day Saturday and all day Sunday they'd been up and down, with hammers and nails, black plastic and bits of wood.

By Sunday evening they'd nailed down the last sheets of plastic on the roof and laid branches across the top. It was big enough for them all to sit in comfortably, and they'd hidden it so well that you wouldn't even know it was there unless you went right up close.

Wallaby reached it first, but he waited for Hero. Though no one ever said so, everyone knew she was the boss. Hero went inside but she was out again almost straight away.

'What's wrong?' said Wallaby. He could tell by the look on her face that something had happened.

'Someone's been in,' said Hero, quietly.

'Aw, don't tell me they've wrecked it!' said Toffer, running towards them, panting, clutching an empty biscuit packet. He'd go crazy if the place had been trashed after all his hard work. Especially carting the old sofa all the way up The Mountain with Hero's Dad.

'No, they haven't wrecked it,' said Hero, angrily. 'But you can smell they've been here.'

Toffer and Wallaby crawled inside. The place stank of beer and cigarettes. 'Yuk!' said the two boys together.

'It must be our Kev and his gang,' said Wallaby. 'Maybe they followed us.' Kev was Wallaby's older brother. None of them liked him much.

'Yeah, maybe,' said Hero. 'See what you can find out, Wallaby.'

The next day was the same. And the day after. First thing they had to do every time they went up was to clear out the bottles and fag-ends, but the smell still wouldn't go away. Hero started bringing a can of air freshener with her to get rid of the stink. Somehow the Den wasn't the same now someone else was using it, someone who kept messing it up.

Speedy he might be, but courage wasn't Wallaby's strong point. It took him till Friday morning to get round to asking his big brother what he'd been up to.

'Kev?' he said at last over breakfast.

'Uh?' Kev scowled into his cornflakes.

'Where were you last night, Kev?'

'What's it to you, kid?'

'Just wondered,' said Wallaby.

'Well you can keep wondering, little brother.' Kev looked up from his bowl, giving Wallaby the evil eye. 'What I do is my business and no one else's. Right?'

'Right,' said Wallaby, showing sudden interest in the dinosaur on the back of the cereal packet.

'Did you ask him?' said Hero, when Wallaby came to call for her before school.

'Yeah.'

'And what did he say?'

'Nothing.'

'Ah.' Hero knew what Kev was like, too. 'Fair enough. We'll have to find out some other way.'

They had a long talk about it at dinner time. 'I'm not so sure it is Kev,' said Hero. 'If it was, he'd have completely wrecked the place by now. Trouble is, whoever's going up there is doing it late on, after we're all back home. So how do we find out who it is?'

'Why don't we stay up in The Woods late and see?' suggested Toffer.

The other two looked at him. 'Reason number one,' said Hero, 'because we're not allowed. Reason number two, because I wouldn't feel safe up there in the dark . . .'

'And reason number three,' added Wallaby, 'because if it is our Kev, I don't want to be around when he finds out he's being spied on.'

Chapter 2

'Dad,' said Hero after school on Friday. 'Someone's been using our Den. What should we do about it?'

Mr Llewelyn looked up from his paper. 'Adult or child?'

'I'm not sure,' Hero answered. 'But they've been smoking and drinking up there. The place stinks.'

'That's a shame,' said her father, putting his paper down. 'Tomorrow's Saturday,' he said, after a while, 'so maybe they'll go up during the day. Why don't the three of you keep an eye on the place? Come back and tell me as soon as you see anyone and I'll go and sort it out. But make sure they don't see you.'

So at eight the next morning Hero and Wallaby called for Toffer.

'Wakey, wakey, Toff,' said Hero, when he finally came to the door, half asleep. 'We're going on an intruder hunt.'

Wallaby was full of bounce as usual. He and Hero raced each other up The Mountain. Wallaby won. He tip-toed to the doorway, peeped in, and ran back to find Hero.

'He's there!'

'Who's there?'

'The man.'

'What man?'

'Don't know.'

'Did he see you?'

'Don't think so.'

'What's he doing?'

'Sleeping.'

They waited for Toffer and then all three of them tip-toed to the den and poked their heads round the doorway to have a look at him.

He was old, with long hair, a straggly beard and tatty clothes, half covered in newspapers. The ground all around him was littered with empty beer bottles and cigarette butts.

'Yuk!' said Hero, Toffer and Wallaby, under their breath.

The man was snoring loudly. As they watched, his whole body shook with a long bout of coughing. They were sure it would wake him up, but it didn't.

'Well it's not your Kev, anyway,' said Hero, when they were back outside. 'Anyone seen him before?'

No one had.

'What'll we do about him?' asked Toffer.

'I know what I'd like to do,' said Hero. 'Wake him up right now and tell him to clear off out of our Den. But you can't be too careful with strangers. I'm going to go and get Dad.'

Then she had a thought. 'Either of you two got a pen and paper?'

Wallaby had the stub of an old pencil in his pocket and Toffer found a shopping list his Mam had given him the night before.

'Dear Sir,' Hero wrote on the other side, 'This is OUR DEN. Please find somewhere else to sleep.'

She underlined OUR DEN four times, and they all signed it. Toffer reached in and put the note on the packing crate so the man wouldn't miss it and they headed for home.

'WAAAAAH!' yelled Toffer, when they got to the edge of The Wood.

'What did you do that for?' asked Hero, right next to him. 'I nearly jumped out of my skin.'

'To wake him up, of course,' said Toffer. 'So he'll be gone when we get back!'

After lunch they returned up The Mountain with Hero's Dad.

'I'll go in first,' Mr Llewelyn told them on the way. 'You lot stay well back till I see if he's still here.'

'Anyone in?' he called from outside. No answer.

He listened by the doorway. No snoring or coughing.

He poked his head through the gap and out again. 'Whoever it was, he's gone,' he told them.

'Good,' said the others, piling in past him.

The bottles had gone too, though not the cigarette butts. And there on the packing crate was Toffer's shopping list, with some writing underneath.

Toffer grabbed it. 'Want to hear what it says?'

Hero and Wallaby nodded.

'Right,' he said importantly, jumping up onto the crate. The other two held their breath, wondering if the box would take Toffer's weight. 'One carton milk, large tin beans, giant box cereal, six packets of chocolate biscuits . . .' He couldn't keep going for giggles.

'Stop being silly, Toffer!' said Hero, crossly. 'This is serious.'

'Oh, all right then,' he said, turning the note over. 'Hey, this writing's awful! "Deer hero toffer and wallaby," I think it says, "sorry for staying in your den without askin didn't mean no harm back later to say sorry singed eli whittlestick".'

'Singed?' said Wallaby.

'I think he means signed,' said Hero. 'Funny name, though, Eli Whittlestick. I wonder what he's like. Who thinks we should be here to meet him? As long as Dad's willing to stay, of course.'

'Yeah, I'm for it,' answered Toffer, still holding the note. 'I've never met anyone whose writing's worse than mine! What do you say, Wallaby?'

'I'm not so sure,' said Wallaby. 'We don't know anything about him.'

'What do you think, Dad?' asked Hero. Her father was outside, sitting on the grass.

But he'd been listening in. 'Eli Whittlestick . . .' he murmured, rubbing his chin thoughtfully. 'Now where have I heard that name before?'

Then, 'Got it!' he said. 'Eli the Woodcarver! He used to come calling round Pentre back when I was a lad.'

'Was that in the time of Owain Glyndŵr, Mr Llewelyn?' asked Toffer, with a grin.

'Don't be so cheeky, you!' Hero's Dad smiled. 'No, I'm sure it's him. Young fellow in his twenties he was when I first met him. Brilliant carver. Comes from an old gypsy family. We used to spend hours together, just chatting about this and that.'

'So is it O.K. for us to meet him without you then?' asked Hero.

'Oh yes,' said her Dad. 'Eli wouldn't hurt a fly. One of the gentlest men I ever met. He always used to drop by whenever he was in town, but I haven't seen him for a few years. I often wondered what happened to him.'

Chapter 3

So at two o'clock Hero, Toffer and Wallaby were waiting in the Den when Eli pushed his way through the doorway. He looked a lot bigger now he wasn't lying down. When he tried to stand up his long dark hair was pressed flat to his head by the roof and they all had to back into the corner to give him room.

'Hello, there,' he said, sitting down on the packing crate and pulling out a cigarette packet. 'I'm Eli.'

Straight away the gang wished he wasn't there, despite what Hero's Dad had said. He seemed to fill the Den, to leave no space for them. He reeked of socks, beer and cigarettes.

'You're not allowed smoke in here!' said Hero. 'It's dangerous.'

'And smelly,' said Wallaby, under his breath.

'Oh, sorry,' said the man. 'I didn't think.' He looked surprised and a bit hurt, but he put the packet back into the pocket of his torn overcoat. 'Let's start again. I'm Eli,' and he held out his hand. They all stared at the filthy palm, the brown cigarette-stained fingers and the broken black nails.

'Yuk!' whispered Wallaby.

'Cool!' muttered Toffer.

'I'm Hero,' announced Hero, grasping his hand.

'Like I said in the note,' Eli told them, perched on the edge of the packing crate, 'I'm sorry for using your den without asking. It was cold and wet and I'd nowhere else to go. I'd like you to take these as a thank you present.'

He reached into his tatty old bag and pulled out

three carved wooden figures, handing them one each.

Hero examined hers. 'Hey, these are great!' she said after a while. 'Did you make them yourself?'

'Certainly did,' said Eli. 'My grandfather taught me when I was about your age. It's how I make a living, walking the roads and selling them to people. That and doing a few odd jobs here and there. These are only spares that didn't quite work out. If you've got time I could make one of you three. As a thank you, like, for letting me stay.'

'Would you really?' said Hero, unable to hide her enthusiasm.

So Eli reached into his bag and pulled out a big lump of wood and a knife, and the gang spent the rest of the afternoon on the sofa, while Eli sat on the packing crate, carving. And as he carved he told them his story.

'My father used to travel the roads,' he began, 'and his before him, as far back as anyone knows. Never stayed in one place more than a few weeks, nowhere you'd really call a home. Though there were places we'd go back to the same time every year, to meet up with the others.'

'So have you never lived in a house?' asked Toffer, amazed.

'Never,' said Eli. 'But I wasn't always walking, like I am now. When we were young we had a horse-drawn caravan. I loved Dimple, that was our mare, more than anything. But in the end she was too old for the job, and she had to go out to pasture.'

'Couldn't you get another one?' asked Hero.

'No,' said Eli. 'Dad said the roads were getting too busy. Said it wasn't fair on the horses any more. So we got a motor caravan instead. It was never the same.'

'Is that why you took to walking?' said Wallaby. 'Bit of a slow way to get about, isn't it?'

'Oh, people are in too much of a hurry these days,' said Eli. 'Rather be out in the fresh air, me, where you can see things properly. Never could stand the smell of petrol, either. Only time I miss having a roof over my head is when I'm feeling poorly, like now with this cough. That's why I wanted to hole up in your den here for a few nights, just till it cleared up.'

'But what about the winter?' asked Hero. 'It must be awful then.'

'It's not so bad, you know. You get used to it, sleeping in barns, old railway carriages, that sort of thing. If it gets really cold I track down the vans and stay with one of my people for a while. But I can't stand being cooped up for too long.'

'What do you eat, though?' asked Toffer, his stomach rumbling at the very thought. 'No microwave, no takeaways, no chocolate biscuits.'

'Oh, I do all right,' said Eli. 'There's places to get food if you know where to go. And people are kind. Sometimes.'

He carried on carving, broken only by occasional bouts of coughing. But Wallaby was getting restless. He kept twitching and scratching.

'I can see how you got your name, young Wallaby,' said Eli, smiling. 'I could never stay still when I was your age, either. But it's a bit difficult doing this with you bouncing about like a kangaroo. Just a few more minutes and I'll be done.'

'Come to think of it,' he added, a short while later, 'Wallaby's not the only odd name round here. What does Toffer mean?'

'It's short for Chris,' answered Toffer, laughing.

'I see,' said Eli, not quite sure he did. 'And what about . . ?' He turned to Hero.

'Hero's just Hero,' said Toffer and Wallaby together. 'Because she's a hero.'

'Ah!' said Eli. This time everyone laughed.

Chapter 4

'Eli,' said Hero, 'how come we haven't seen you around town, if you make your living knocking on doors?'

'Well, no offence like,' answered Eli, looking up from his carving. 'But I'm afraid I gave up on Pentre a while ago. Used to be real friendly in the old days, people inviting you in for meals and all that, but it's changed. Last time I was here, oh about three or four years ago, a gang of kids chased me out of town. Swearing, chucking tins, that sort of thing. Puts you off a place, it does.'

'I bet it does,' said Hero. 'But I can't believe that happened here.'

'I can,' muttered Wallaby, thinking of big brother Kev and the gang.

'It's not the worst by any means,' Eli went on. 'You've always had some people wary of travelling folk, but there's towns I have to avoid completely these days. All you get is dirty looks, or worse.' He coughed again. 'Not that I'd live any other way.'

'So how did you find The Den if you didn't want to go anywhere near Pentre?' asked Wallaby.

'I was on my way to Aber,' answered Eli,

'skirting the edge of town, when I saw it. It was just getting dark and I had this cold coming on, so I was looking for a place to rest up. Well hidden it was, I'll say that for you lot, but Old Eli can spot a good shelter a mile off.'

'So have you tried Pentre since you've been up at The Den, then?' asked Hero.

'Oh, I've knocked on one or two doors,' answered Eli. 'It's not been so bad this time, I'll admit. No sign of those hooligans, not so far, anyway. But Pentre's not a good place for me any more. Once Old Eli makes up his mind about somewhere it takes a lot to change it.'

He returned to his carving. The children shuffled uncomfortably.

'Eli . . .' said Hero after a time. 'Have you ever been to school?'

'No,' he answered. 'Never set foot in one. Don't like that sort of a place. Try to make everyone the same, far as I can see.'

'But Eli . . .' she asked, puzzled, 'you understood my note and you wrote an answer. How did you learn to read and write if you never went to school?'

'Oh, that was my mother. She wasn't from a travelling family, see. Lived down in the Valleys, till my father came calling. Ran off with him, she

27

did. She's the one that taught me. I'm not great at writing, but I can get by if I have to. Rather use my hands for carving, any day.'

'There you are!' he said, a few minutes later. 'All done.'

He blew the last wood shavings off and handed it to Toffer. It was all three of them, Hero, Toffer and Wallaby, side by side on the sofa, cut out of the one bit of wood.

'Wow!' said Toffer. 'That's brilliant, Eli. It's just like us!'

And so it was. From Wallaby's long gangly legs to Hero's plaits, even down to Toffer's chubby cheeks and spiky hair.

'Thanks, Eli,' said Hero, turning it round and round slowly, looking at all the perfect little details. 'It's lovely.'

'Eli . . .' she said after a minute, a plan forming in her head. 'Would you mind if I took it into school to show our teacher, Miss Parry?'

'Mmm, I don't know about that,' said Eli.

'Oh please,' she begged. 'I know you don't

think much of schools, but they're not like they were in your day. Well, ours isn't anyway. And Miss Parry's great. She'd love your carving.'

'Oh, all right,' said Eli, grudgingly. 'But only if you promise not to leave it there.'

As they were about to go, the three children got into a huddle.

'Eli,' said Hero, breaking away, 'we've had a talk, and we've agreed that now you're our friend you can stay in The Den as long as you like.'

'That's very nice of you,' said Eli, tugging his beard thoughtfully, 'but like I said before, I think it's time to be moving on.'

'Please, Eli,' said Hero. 'At least until your cold's cleared up.'

Eli thought for a while. And had another fit of coughing.

'Oh, all right then,' he decided. 'Maybe it's not such a bad idea. Just for another day or two. Thanks.'

So they left him in The Den and headed off home, talking the whole way back.

'We've got to do something, Hero,' said Wallaby.

'Yeah,' said Toffer. 'It's horrible the way Eli thinks everyone in Pentre's so unfriendly, especially the kids. How can we make him see what it's really like?'

'Ah . . .' said Hero, with that funny look in her eye that they knew meant she was up to something. 'That's what I'm working on.'

Chapter 5

That evening Wallaby was up in his room, doing his homework, when he heard shouting from outside. He looked out of the window and saw Eli shambling down the street, with Kev and the gang following along behind, taunting him.

'Clear out, you smelly gippo!' yelled Kev, chucking a coke tin at him. The can hit Eli on the back and the sticky liquid ran all the way down his coat.

Before he had time to think, Wallaby had opened the window and was shouting, 'Leave him alone, you big bully!'

Looking round to find out who dared challenge him, Kev was horrified to see it was his kid brother. The rest of the gang were pointing at Wallaby, laughing, and Kev's face turned bright red. As he raced into the house, no one noticed Eli take the opportunity to disappear up a side street.

'I'll get you for that, kid!' Kev shouted, pounding up the stairs.

Wallaby ran down the landing and hid in the bathroom. When Kev burst into Wallaby's room, the younger boy shot down the stairs, out onto the

street, past the gang who were still rolling about in fits of laughter, and dashed up to Hero's house.

'Let me in, let me in!' he yelled, banging on the door. Luckily Hero was in the hallway, on the phone. She opened up and Wallaby slipped inside, just as Kev reappeared on his doorstep.

'Where's that brother of mine? Wait till I get my hands on him!' said Kev, but the gang shrugged their shoulders.

'Didn't see no one,' said the first.

'Must've gone out the back,' said another. But they were having trouble not laughing, and Kev could see it.

'Ah, forget him!' said Kev, stomping off down the street. 'He's only a stupid kid. Not worth bothering about anyway.'

'Aren't you coming, then?' he shouted, when he'd got to the corner. But for some reason the rest of the gang stayed where they were.

Meanwhile Wallaby was gasping for breath in Hero's front room, and trying to tell her all about it at the same time.

'I'm proud of you, Wallaby,' said Hero, when she worked out what had happened. 'That's probably the bravest thing you've ever done.'

'And the stupidest,' said Wallaby.

'Oh, I'm not so sure,' said Hero, keeping half

an eye on what was going on outside. 'The only reason that lot hang around with your Kev is because they're scared of him. I bet they were glad to see someone stand up to him for once. Maybe he'll calm down a bit, now he knows the gang won't always back him up.'

'Hmm, I'm not so sure,' said Wallaby. 'Do you think I could stay here for the night, just in case?'

So Hero's Dad rang Wallaby's Mam, who gave Kev a good talking to when he came back in. Wallaby stayed the night at Hero's, went home the next morning, and didn't see any sign of Kev all day. And though big brother had a permanent scowl on his face for the next week and a half, nothing more was said.

Chapter 6

If there was one thing Miss Parry, their teacher, loved more than anything else, it was Art. More than Maths, more than Biology, even more than Music. Every time they had an Art lesson, and they seemed to have one at least once a day, she'd start off by showing them Some Famous Picture and ask them what they thought of it. They'd try to think of something sensible to say and then she'd be off. About how Wonderful it was and how she'd been to see it in some World Famous Art Gallery in France or Italy in the summer holidays and how it was the High Point of her Life.

Some of them thought she was a bit of a nutter but they all rather liked her, even though she was a bit strict sometimes. So nobody laughed. And all that art did seem to make you look at things differently.

These days she was on about Sculpture. Rodin, Michaelangelo, that lot. They'd been on a trip down to St. David's the week before, where she pointed out Every Fascinating Feature.

So when she said on Monday morning, 'I'm going to pass round a picture of one of my favourite sculptures, and then we're going to have a go at making one out of clay,' there were one or two quiet groans before Hero stuck up her hand.

'Please, Miss . . .'

'Yes, Hermione.'

'Please, Miss, I've got a sort of little sculpture I'd like to show the class. It's here in my bag.'

'Oh, lovely,' said Miss Parry. 'Bring it up, then.'

The class watched as Hero pulled the carving out and carried it to the teacher's desk. Miss Parry was silent for a full two minutes, examining it.

'Hermione,' she said at last, 'this is beautiful! It's you, Christopher and Gwilym, isn't it?'

'Yes, Miss,' said Hero, proudly. Toffer and Wallaby were beaming too.

'But who on earth made it?' asked the teacher.

'Eli Whittlestick,' answered Hero. 'He's a friend of my dad. He travels the roads.'

There were a few giggles from the back, but Miss Parry fixed them with an icy glare. 'Can I pass it round the class, Hermione?'

Hero nodded.

'Be VERY careful with it, everyone!' said the teacher. And she handed it down to the children at the front.

'Hermione . . .' said Miss Parry later, when they were all up to their armpits in clay. 'Do you think your Eli would come into school to talk about his life on the roads, and maybe show us how he makes his lovely carvings?'

'I'm not sure, Miss Parry,' Hero answered. 'I'm afraid he doesn't like schools much. He says they try to make everyone the same. And he doesn't like Pentre now, either. Says it's unfriendly.'

Miss Parry called Hero back at the end of the day. 'I've had a word with Mr Jones, Hermione.' Mr Jones was the head teacher. 'He was very interested in what you had to tell me, and he says that if Eli came in to talk to the class he'd be very happy to give him a small donation from the school funds. What do you think? Could you get him to do it?'

'I'm not sure, Miss,' said Hero, smiling. 'But I'll try.'

She skipped home, pleased as punch. Her plan was working.

Chapter 7

So at half-past eight the next morning, when Hero's dad opened the front door expecting to see only Wallaby as usual, he was very pleased to find his old friend Eli Whittlestick too.

Wallaby ran inside, leaving Eli and Hero's Dad to have a chat about old times.

'Drop by later, Eli,' said Mr Llewelyn, when Hero and Wallaby had reappeared on the doorstep. He realised they were itching to get away and planning to take Eli with them. 'I want to hear all your news.'

They headed off up the road to pick up Toffer. Hero could see that Eli was nervous by the way he was tugging at his beard.

'Don't worry, Eli,' she said. 'Nobody messes about in Miss Parry's class. And she thinks your carvings are great.'

There were one or two giggles when Eli walked in, but a long hard stare from Miss Parry soon sorted them out. And once Eli started talking about his childhood you could have heard a pin drop.

When he'd finished, the teacher asked if anyone had any questions for him, and they poured in from all sides.

'What happened to Dimple?'

'Is Whittlestick your real name?'

'*Ydych chi'n siarad Cymraeg?*' (Do you speak Welsh?)

'Why don't you like schools?'

'What's your e-mail address?'

'Can I borrow your knife to sharpen my pencil?'

'How do you survive without a television?'

'Don't you get lonely living on your own?'

'How often do you have a bath?'

'Who chased you out of Pentre?'

'What do you do in the winter?'

There were so many questions, it would have gone on all morning if the bell hadn't rung for break.

Then when they came back inside, Miss Parry divided the class into three.

Wallaby's group had to discuss whether Eli was right to think Pentre was an unfriendly town.

Toffer chose to talk about whether it was right to judge somebody just by how they looked. He'd always been fed up with people thinking he was stupid just because he was a bit on the large side, so he soon set them straight on that one.

And Hero's group were talking about whether

school really tried to make everyone think the same way, and whether that was a good idea.

The room was a complete buzz. And when it was time for Hero and Toffer to report back, everyone had something to add, even little Cerys Thomas who never said a word. Eli sat at the back and listened, amazed.

And then while they wrote poems and stories, imaging themselves as travellers, Eli took out his whittling knife, selected a suitable bit of wood, and began to carve a likeness of Miss Parry, who was so excited she could hardly sit still.

Eli sat with the children for dinner and then said he had to be off. But before he could go, the other teachers, who'd heard all about the morning's activities from Miss Parry, pleaded with him not to leave town without spending some time in each of their classes, too.

The children went home full of tales of Eli, and lots of the parents sent messages through the school that they'd be glad to have him come knocking.

So Eli spent a whole two weeks more in Pentre, doing jobs and selling carvings. He had a school dinner every lunchtime, a hot meal with a different set of parents every night, more baths than he'd had in a year, and his cold got completely better.

On his last day in school Mr Jones, the Headteacher, called Eli into his office and gave him a letter to show to the junior school anywhere he passed through, saying that if they had a few pounds to spare, Eli Whittlestick was an excellent speaker.

'So what do you think of Pentre now?' Hero asked Eli up at The Den on Saturday, as Toffer polished off the last of their farewell picnic.

'Oh, it's not so bad . . .' said Eli. 'I'll tell you one thing, I haven't eaten so well in years. And I've learned a few things, too.'

'Like what?' said Hero.

'Like not to give up on places so quickly,' said Eli, with a grin. 'And that maybe schools aren't so bad, after all.'

'So will you be back?' said Wallaby.

'I should think I might,' said Eli, smiling. 'No promises, like. You can't tie Old Eli down that easy. But I'd imagine round about this time next year I just might stop off to see whether The Den's still here. And maybe look up two or three young friends.'

And with that he picked up his bag, shook

Hero, Toffer and Wallaby each by the hand, and strode off down The Mountain.

They watched him disappear from view before Wallaby turned to Hero.

'It all worked out, didn't it, Hero? You knew if we could get Eli into school that Pentre would like him and he'd like Pentre, didn't you?'

Hero nodded.

'You're the hero again, aren't you, Hero?' said Toffer, laughing.

'Oh I don't know about that,' said Hero, looking over at Wallaby. 'I'm not the one who stood up to Kev.'

'Or the one who convinced the class that you shouldn't judge people just by how they look,' said Wallaby, smiling at Toffer.

'So maybe we're all heroes,' said Hero.

'Yeah, maybe we are,' said the other two, nodding their heads. 'Maybe we are.'

About the author . . .

It took me forty years to become a writer. Forty years of packing Polo mints, selling coffee, teaching kids. Of raising children, cats and goats and pigs.

I live in Aberdyfi now, in a big old house overlooking the Irish sea. It reminds me of the one I grew up in, near Belfast.

I like Wales. I like being a writer. I hope you like my story.

Malachy